SECRET AGENT

The Puzzle of the Missing Panda: CHINA

Join Secret Agent Jack Stalwart

on his other adventures:

The Search for the Sunken Treasure: **AUSTRALIA**

The Secret of the Sacred Temple: **CAMBODIA**

The Mystery of the Mona Lisa: **FRANCE**

The Caper of the Crown Jewels: **GREAT BRITAIN**

Peril at the Grand Prix: **ITALY**

The Pursuit of the Ivory Poachers: **KENYA**

The Escape of the Deadly Dinosaur: **USA**

The Puzzle
of the
Missing Panda:
CHINA

Elizabeth Singer Hunt

Illustrated by Brian Williamson

RED FOX

THE PUZZLE OF THE MISSING PANDA: CHINA
A RED FOX BOOK 978 1 862 30475 8

First published in Great Britain by Chubby Cheeks Publications Limited
Published in this edition by Red Fox,
an imprint of Random House Children's Books
A Random House Group Company

Chubby Cheeks edition published 2004
This edition published 2007

Text copyright © Elizabeth Singer Hunt 2004, 2007
Illustrations copyright © Brian Williamson, 2007, adapted from the original
Jack Stalwart illustrations © Elizabeth Singer Hunt, 2004–5

The Random House Group Limited makes every effort to ensure that the papers used
in its books are from trees that have been legally sourced from well-managed and
credibly certified forests. Our paper procurement policy can be found at
www.randomhouse.co.uk/paper.htm

 **Mixed Sources**
Product group from well-managed
forests and other controlled sources
www.fsc.org Cert no. TT-COC-2139
© 1996 Forest Stewardship Council
FSC

Set in Meta, Trixie, American Typewriter, Luggagetag, Gill Sans Condensed
and Serpentine.

Red Fox Books are published by Random House Children's Books,
61–63 Uxbridge Road, London W5 5SA

www.kidsatrandomhouse.co.uk

Addresses for companies within The Random House Group Limited can be found at:
www.randomhouse.co.uk/offices.htm

THE RANDOM HOUSE GROUP Limited Reg. No. 954009

A CIP catalogue record for this book is available from the British Library.

Printed in the UK by CPI Bookmarque, Croydon, CR0 4TD

For Ann and Robert Hunt

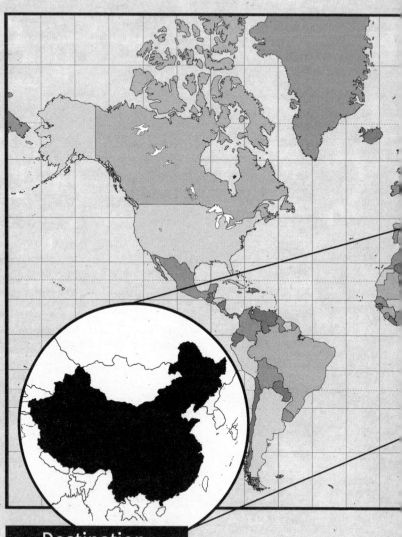

Destination:
CHINA

My name is Jack Stalwart. My older brother,

Max, was a secret agent for you, until he

disappeared on one of your missions. Now I

want to be a secret agent too. If you choose

me, I will be an excellent secret agent and get

rid of evil villains, just like my brother did.

Sincerely,

Jack Stalwart

THINGS YOU'LL FIND IN EVERY BOOK

Watch Phone: The only gadget Jack wears all the time, even when he's not on official business. His Watch Phone is the central gadget that makes most others work. There are lots of important features, most importantly the 'C' button, which reveals the code of the day – necessary to unlock Jack's Secret Agent Book Bag. There are buttons on both sides, one of which ejects his life-saving Melting Ink Pen. Beyond these functions, it also works as a phone and, of course, gives Jack the time of day.

Global Protection Force (GPF): The GPF is the organization Jack works for. It's a worldwide force of young secret agents whose aim is to protect the world's people, places and possessions. No one knows exactly where its main offices are located (all correspondence and gadgets for repair are sent to a special PO Box, and training is held at various locations around the world), but Jack thinks it's somewhere cold, like the Arctic Circle.

Whizzy: Jack's magical miniature globe. Almost every night at precisely 7:30 p.m., the GPF uses Whizzy to send Jack the identity of the country that he must travel to. Whizzy can't talk, but he can cough up messages. Jack's parents don't know Whizzy is anything more than a normal globe.

The Magic Map: The magical map hanging on Jack's bedroom wall. Unlike most maps, the GPF's map is made of a mysterious wood. Once Jack inserts the country piece from Whizzy, the map swallows Jack whole and sends him away on his missions. When he returns, he arrives precisely one minute after he left.

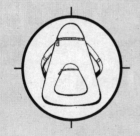

Secret Agent Book Bag: The Book Bag that Jack wears on every adventure. Licensed only to GPF secret agents, it contains top-secret gadgets necessary to foil bad guys and escape certain death. To activate the bag before each mission, Jack must punch in a secret code given to him by his Watch Phone. Once he's away, all he has to do is place his finger on the zip, which identifies him as the owner of the bag and immediately opens.

THE STALWART FAMILY

Jack's dad, John

He moved the family to England when Jack was two, in order to take a job with an aerospace company. As far as Jack knows, his dad designs and manufactures aeroplane parts. Jack's dad thinks he is an ordinary boy and that his other son, Max, attends a school in Switzerland. Jack's dad is American and his mum is British, which makes Jack a bit of both.

Jack's mum, Corinne

One of the greatest mums as far as Jack is concerned. When she and her husband received a letter from a posh school in Switzerland inviting Max to attend, they were overjoyed. Since Max left six months ago, they have received numerous notes in Max's handwriting telling them he's OK. Little do they know it's all a lie and that it's the GPF sending those letters.

Jack's older brother, Max

Two years ago, at the age of nine, Max joined the GPF. Max used to tell Jack about his adventures and show him how to work his secret-agent gadgets. When the family received a letter inviting Max to attend a school in Europe, Jack figured it was to do with the GPF. Max told him he was right, but that he couldn't tell Jack anything about why he was going away.

Nine-year-old Jack Stalwart

Four months ago, Jack received an anonymous note saying: 'Your brother is in danger. Only you can save him.' As soon as he could, Jack applied to be a secret agent too. Since that time, he's battled some of the world's most dangerous villains, and hopes some day in his travels to find and rescue his brother, Max.

DESTINATION:
China

Most people make their living as farmers. They grow lots of things, including rice, corn, sweet potatoes and peanuts

●

China is located on the continent of Asia

●

Beijing (pronounced *bay-jing*) is its capital city

●

It's the third largest country in the world. One out of every five people on Earth live in China

Chinese people use symbols instead of letters in their writing. There are over 40,000 Chinese symbols

●

China's official currency is the Yuan

●

Mandarin is the official language, although lots of other languages are spoken

GIANT PANDA: FACTS AND FIGURES

More Giant Pandas live in China than anywhere else in the world

The Chinese name for the Giant Panda means 'large bear cat'

Pandas mainly eat bamboo, although they like eggs, honey and insects too

Since their digestion is poor, they eat for up to twelve hours a day

Panda paws have five fingers and one thumb

The main threat to the Giant Panda is the loss of habitat due to logging and human development

THE TERRACOTTA ARMY: FACTS AND FIGURES

The Terracotta Army is not a real army, but a collection of over 8,000 clay statues made to look like real officers and soldiers

They were commissioned by the first emperor of unified China, Qin Shi Huang, and placed near his tomb when he died in 210 BC

The statues were discovered in 1974 near Xi'an by a man drilling for water

The army is organized into three 'pits': the main army, the military guard and the command unit

No two soldiers are the same. Each has a different face and uniform

The emperor's tomb itself remains sealed

SECRET AGENT GADGET INSTRUCTION MANUAL

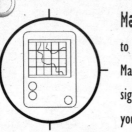

Map Mate: When you're lost or need to get somewhere fast, use the GPF's Map Mate. This clever gadget receives signals from satellites in space to give you a map of any city or town in the world. It can also show you how to get from one place to another using directional arrows to guide the way.

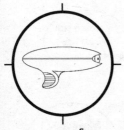

Laser Burst: The GPF's Laser Burst is a handheld laser that emits a powerful white light capable of slicing through almost anything. Perfect when you need to burn a quick hole, start a camp fire or cut through something hard.

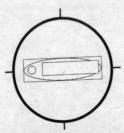

Secret Language Decoder: When you need to figure out what someone or something is saying, use the GPF's Secret Language Decoder.

To decipher foreign text, push the 'read' button. To translate speech, push 'listen' and wait for the translation to appear on the screen.

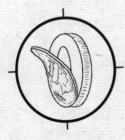

Motion Sensor: The GPF's Motion Sensor looks like a coin but it's actually a hi-tech motion-detecting device. Just peel off the fake backing to stick it in place. Once it's attached it will send a signal to your Watch Phone if anything moves within three metres of its range.

Chapter 1:
The Throw

Jack and his mum drove into the village
hall car park. 'I'll pick you up in an hour,'
she said. Jack opened the door, quickly
waved 'goodbye' and shut the door
behind him. His mum had some grocery
shopping to do. She put the car in gear
and pulled away.

Every weekend, twenty kids including
Jack met to learn judo from Mr Baskin,
one of the best judo instructors in Great

Britain. Judo is a type of martial art from Japan. Thanks to Mr Baskin, Jack had already earned his yellow belt. Not only was judo recommended by the GPF, it was something that Jack loved doing.

As he entered the building, he spotted his friends Richard and Charlie. They were also dressed in the judo uniform called a *judogi*. A *judogi* was a white jacket and trousers with a special

belt tied around the waist. Jack walked over to say 'hi', but almost at the same time Mr Baskin yelled out to the class.

'OK, everyone!' he said. 'Let's begin.'

Jack went over to the edge of the mat, tidied up his *judogi* and tossed off his flip-flops. Then he, Richard, Charlie and the rest of the class stepped onto the mat and waited for instructions.

'Floor work!' Mr Baskin said.

'Commando style!' he added.

Everyone knew what to do. Hurrying to one side of the mat, the first row of students dropped to the floor and lay on their stomachs. Then they used their elbows to pull themselves across the mat, like soldiers in a trench. Almost as soon as they'd finished, Mr Baskin shouted another command.

'Cartwheels!' he said.

Jack could hear the rest of the boys sigh in dread. While the girls in the class loved doing cartwheels, it was difficult for Jack and the other boys to get their legs round.

Jack did his best, and when he'd made it across the mat, he heard Mr Baskin call everyone back to the centre. They returned to the middle, sat back on their heels and listened carefully to what the teacher had to say.

'Can anyone tell me what *hansoku-make* means?' he asked.

Jack knew the answer. He raised his hand. 'Disqualification,' he offered when Mr Baskin called on him.

'Yes!' said Mr Baskin, pleased that the first answer of the day was a correct one. 'And what causes a disqualification?' he asked.

Charlie's hand shot up. 'Putting your fingers up an opponent's sleeve,' he answered.

'Well,' said Mr Baskin, 'that wouldn't cause a *hansoku-make*. Can anyone tell me what putting your hands up an opponent's sleeve *would* cause?'

Richard raised his hand. 'A *shido*?'

'Excellent!' Mr Baskin said. 'Yes, putting your fingers up someone's sleeve would cause a *shido*, or small penalty.

'What else?' he asked, searching for other means of disqualification.

A girl a few kids back from Jack raised her hand. Although Jack didn't know her name, he knew that she was more skilled than him because she was wearing an orange belt.

'Punching someone in the face,' she replied, with a naughty smile.

The instructor smiled back. 'Good one, Charlotte,' he said. 'Any other ideas?'

Charlie raised his hand again. 'What about if you wear metal or jewellery?' he asked.

'Yes!' said Mr Baskin, excited that his class had been paying attention to previous lessons.

Another girl raised her hand too. Jack recognized her as Emma, a girl who lived a few streets over from him. She was eight years old.

'Biting someone?' she offered.

'Excellent,' said Mr Baskin. 'All of those things – punching, wearing metal and biting – can lead to disqualification.

'Now,' he continued, moving on from the questions and answers, 'today, we're going to learn a new throw. It's called a harai goshi. It's known as the "sweeping hip throw" and is an excellent move that can have a number of results.'

He got up and, with the help of Tim, a thirteen-year-old boy who sometimes assisted him, showed the class how it was done. When the demonstration was over, the instructor told everyone to find a partner. Richard and Charlie nabbed each other first, which left Jack alone, but not for long. Charlotte, the girl with the orange belt, turned up in front of him almost instantly.

'Wanna be my partner?' she asked.

Jack looked around for another partner, but everyone had already paired up. He never liked practising with girls. He didn't like the thought of hurting them.

'OK,' he said reluctantly. 'Shall we get started?'

Jack and Charlotte bowed to each other. As Jack reached for Charlotte's sleeve, she moved quickly. She grabbed his right arm, twisted in towards his body, lifted him up on her back, then grabbed his trouser leg and threw him on the floor.

THWACK!

Jack's body hit the mat hard. He'd never been thrown by a girl before. He looked up at Charlotte, who was standing above him, arms crossed, with one of those know-it-all grins on her face. Hopefully his friends hadn't seen what had happened.

Pretending that it didn't bother him, Jack got up and coolly said, 'I let you do that.'

He and Charlotte faced each other for another match. As they tidied their *judogis*, Jack was going through the moves in his head. Just as they were about to begin, Mr Baskin shouted for everyone to find a new partner. Without saying a word, Charlotte flicked her ponytail and strutted off with her nose in the air.

Before Jack could think about getting back at Charlotte, Adam stepped in front of him. He and Adam were in the same class at school. The two of them bowed to each other, and after a pretty good wrestle, Jack threw Adam to the floor. Then they repeated the move and Jack let Adam do the same to him.

They practised over and over, so that
by the end of that session, Jack was
pretty good at performing the *harai goshi*.
Now all he had to do was find Charlotte
again. He'd throw *her* this time round. But
unfortunately that wasn't going to happen
– at least, not today.

'Gather up!' yelled Mr Baskin,
motioning for everyone to sit in front of
him in a row.

Jack and the rest of the students sat on their heels across from Mr Baskin, who congratulated them on their hard work. As soon as they were dismissed, Jack, Richard and Charlie gathered up their things and walked outside.

While they were waiting for their mums, they talked about lots of things, like whether they were going to enter the next judo competition. (Richard was, Charlie wasn't and Jack thought he might.)

When Jack's mum pulled up, Jack said goodbye to his friends and climbed into the car, which was filled with groceries.

When he got home, he helped his mum put away the food and then played a car-racing game on his Xbox. Sometime after dinner, he kissed his mum goodnight – his dad was working all weekend again – and made his way upstairs to his room.

As he got to his door, Jack flipped the sign outside to 'KEEP OUT'. Although he loved his mum, he didn't want her just barging in. After all, top-secret stuff happened in there. And it was nearly 7:30 p.m.

Chapter 2:
The Deer-Shaped
Country

As soon as Jack shut the door, he looked over at his miniature globe, Whizzy, who was fast asleep. For some reason, seeing Whizzy like this made Jack think about the time they first met. It was at the GPF swearing-in ceremony, when Jack officially became a secret agent.

Ms Pembroke, the lady in charge of globe selection, told Jack to pick one from a long table of globes. As Jack walked by, he noticed that each had a name like

'Zippy' or 'Zoom'. When he came to a little globe called 'Whizzy', he stopped and leaned in for a closer look.

As he did so, the globe smiled, lifted his eyebrows and winked at Jack. Thinking he was cute, Jack picked him up and turned to Ms Pembroke. 'I'll have this one,' he said. And that's how Whizzy came to be in Jack's house that night.

Jack walked over to his friend, just as the time on his Watch Phone ticked over to 7:30 p.m. Almost instantly, Whizzy's eyes popped open. When he saw Jack, he winked and began to spin.

Jack watched as the globe twirled even faster. After a few seconds, Whizzy coughed. *Ahem!* A jigsaw piece in the shape of a country flew out of his mouth. Jack rushed over to pick it up. Whizzy, exhausted from the exercise, fell asleep again.

This one looks like a deer with two antlers, thought Jack as he studied the piece in his hand. Now, let's see where it fits.

Jack carried the piece over to his Magic Map. The Magic Map on his bedroom wall had over 150 countries carved into its special wood. When Jack put the jigsaw piece from Whizzy's mouth in the right spot, the Magic Map transported him to his next mission.

Starting in the upper left corner of the map, Jack slid the piece over every lump and bump. When he crossed over the continent of Europe and passed into the continent of Asia, the piece snapped into place. The word 'CHINA' appeared, then quickly vanished.

'I can't believe it,' said Jack. 'I'm going to China!' Ever since he and his parents started eating at the local Chinese restaurant, Jack had been interested in the food and language of that country.

Knowing that many people in China didn't speak English, Jack figured he needed his Secret Language Decoder. Punching the 'C' button on his Watch Phone, he called up the code of the day.

After receiving the word D-U-M-P-L-I-N-G, he typed it into the lock on his special Book Bag and waited for it to snap open. When it did, he checked the contents inside. Sure enough, his Secret Language Decoder was there, as were his Magic Key Maker, Motion Sensor and Net Tosser.

Closing his bag, Jack slipped his arms through the straps and tightened them over his shoulders. Standing before the Magic Map, he looked at the country of

China. Inside, a small orange light began to glow. It grew until it lit up his entire room.

When the time was right, Jack yelled, 'Off to China!' Then the light flickered and burst, and swallowed him into the Magic Map.

Chapter 3:
The Misty Forest

When Jack opened his eyes, he found himself standing in the middle of a big forest covered in mist and filled with tall stalks of green bamboo. Jack knew that bamboo was a type of grass, not a tree, and that it grew in most parts of Asia.

In his GPF training, he'd learned about the wonders of bamboo. It was light yet strong enough to make lots of things, including rafts (it could float) and ladders. Inside the stalk were tiny worms that could be eaten if you needed food.

Jack had tasted a bamboo worm once. Surprisingly, it didn't taste like a worm, but like peanut butter; one of Jack's favourite foods. Knowing about bamboo was an important skill if you were on assignment in Asia.

As Jack's mind drifted off thinking about the grass, the sound of cracking branches from behind brought things back into focus. Jack quickly turned round to find a small woman dressed in khaki-coloured clothing walking towards him. She looked friendly enough; her eyes were as gentle as her smile.

'*Nǐ hào*,' she said as she approached Jack. '*Wǒ jiào* Mei. It is a pleasure to meet you,' and she bowed her head in Jack's direction.

Guessing she was his contact, Jack bowed his head in respect. '*Wǒ jiào* Jack,' he replied. He decided to see if Mei

spoke English. 'It's a pleasure to meet you too. What can I do for you?'

She nodded to show she understood him. 'A terrible thing has happened,' said Mei, lowering her eyes and shaking her head. 'You are standing in the Wolong Nature Reserve, one of the largest habitats for the endangered Giant Panda. There are only about a thousand Giant Pandas left in the world, and many of them live here in the reserve.

'Last night,' she carried on, 'one of our female pandas, Ling, disappeared. No one knows what happened to her, but I think she was kidnapped. I need you to find Ling and bring her back to the reserve as soon as possible.'

Before Jack could respond, Mei added, 'Time is especially important, as Ling needs bamboo to survive. The longer she is away from the reserve and her bamboo, the more her life is in danger.'

'Don't worry,' said Jack, trying to reassure Mei. 'I'll find Ling and bring her back to you. The first thing I need to do is take a look at where she was last seen.'

'No problem,' answered Mei. 'I will ask Fong, one of our park assistants, to show you around. He should be able to help, since he was assigned to Ling and kept a record of her daily habits.'

'Terrific,' said Jack, who was anxious to start his mission. 'I would love to meet him.'

Chapter 4:
The Hairy Teenager

Mei radioed for Fong to come and join them. Within minutes, the park assistant appeared. When he did, Jack was a bit surprised. He didn't look anything like what he'd expected.

Firstly, Fong wasn't an adult; he was only a teenager. Secondly, he was dressed completely in black. His hair looked like it hadn't been washed in ages and he had a tattoo of a scorpion on the back of his left hand. Out of a mole on

his chin grew a curly black hair that was
so long, Jack couldn't stop staring at it.

'What are you looking at?' Fong
growled. Jack was surprised that he could
speak English.

'Uh . . . Nothing,' said Jack, snapping himself out of it. He quickly extended his hand to Fong. 'Hi, I am here to help find Ling.'

Fong glared at Jack, probably still annoyed that he'd been staring at his mole. He didn't put out his hand to shake Jack's.

'Fong,' said Mei, interrupting the uncomfortable pause, 'why don't you show Jack where Ling was last seen?'

'It would be great if you could,' said Jack. 'There might be something there that would be useful to the investigation.'

For a second Fong stared at Jack. Then he turned his back on him and started walking into the forest.

'You will have to excuse Fong,' said Mei. 'He's a bit shy. He doesn't really say that much. And of course he is worried about Ling.'

'That's all right, Mei,' said Jack politely.
'I meet all kinds of people in this job. I
am sure that Fong and I will get along
great.' As he waved goodbye he added,
'Next time I see you, I will have Ling with
me.'

'I hope so,' said Mei, and she waved
back.

Chapter 5:
The Dirt Road

'So what made you decide to be a park assistant?' Jack asked Fong, trying to make conversation as they trudged through the forest, stepping over fallen branches along the way.

Fong rolled his eyes and continued to walk ahead of Jack. For every step that Fong took, Jack had to take two.

'I mean,' Jack carried on, 'it must be exciting to see the Giant Panda in the wild. I've only ever seen one in a picture or on the Internet. What are they like in real life?'

Fong continued to ignore Jack. It was obvious that he was still upset about his mole. 'Well, I am sure it won't take long to find Ling,' said Jack as they carried on.

Just then, Fong stopped and turned to look at Jack. He stared at him for a few seconds and then pointed to a clearing in the forest. 'Over there,' he muttered.

'Great!' said Jack as he rushed towards the clearing.

It was a large area that had been flattened by the weight of the panda as she was sitting, probably eating bamboo. Around the clearing were broken bits of bamboo grass and fresh animal droppings.

When Jack bent down for a closer look, he didn't notice anything unusual about the bamboo or the poo. But he did see a

path of broken twigs and trodden-on
grass leading from the clearing and to the
right. Perhaps they drugged and then
dragged Ling from this spot, Jack thought.
He followed the trail with his eyes and
saw that it went under some trees.

'Where does that lead?' Jack asked
Fong. Fong raised his eyebrow, shrugged
his shoulders and shook his head as if to
say 'I don't know'.

Motioning for Fong to follow him, Jack quickly but carefully made his way into the woods. As he pushed some hanging branches out of his way, he spied some light peeking through. It was only about ten metres away. There must be another way out, he thought.

Studying the ground as he walked, Jack spotted a square piece of paper. He bent down to pick it up. What he originally thought was a piece of paper was actually a book of matches. Odd, he thought, that something like this would be lying in the middle of the forest.

Since he didn't have time to decipher the Chinese characters that were printed on the outside, he tucked it into his trouser pocket and carried on. For all Jack knew, Ling could still be nearby. He needed to hurry.

The forest stopped at a dirt track that was covered in tyre marks. It looked as though one set had been made recently. To the right, the road ended; to the left, it carried on north. Although the tyre marks in the dirt were fuzzy, Jack had a pretty good idea that the vehicle was some kind of truck.

Jack turned to Fong. 'Whoever took Ling must have loaded her into a truck here,' he explained. 'We need to drive north to see if we can pick up any more clues.'

Fong looked at Jack and then picked up his mobile phone. 'I'll call a friend,' he muttered. He dialled a number and spoke to someone in Chinese. After only ten minutes, a truck pulled up in front of Jack and Fong. The passenger door opened and Jack looked in.

Sitting in the driver's seat was another dark-haired teenage park assistant. He grinned at Jack.

'Hey there,' he said, flashing his teeth. 'I'm Wong. I hear you're looking for Ling. Climb in and we can all look together.'

'Great!' said Jack, pleased that someone else was as interested as he was in finding the panda.

Jack crawled into the back of the truck, while Fong climbed into the front next to Wong. The next thing Jack knew, Wong slammed his foot on the accelerator and the three of them took off, leaving only a flurry of dust circling behind them.

Chapter 6:
The Secret Language

Within minutes of them driving down the
dirt road, Fong reached into a
compartment in the dashboard and pulled
out a packet of cigarettes. He then pulled
a book of matches from his shirt pocket
and lit a cigarette.

After taking a long, extended puff, Fong
rolled down the window and tossed the
empty matchbook out. But the wind from
the speeding truck sent the matchbook
flying into the back and onto Jack's lap.

He picked it up and passed it over the front seat to Fong.

'Excuse me, Fong,' he said. 'This blew back inside.'

'Give me that!' Fong snapped as he turned round and grabbed it from Jack. 'Keep your hands off my things.'

Jack sat back in his seat, in a state of shock. Why was Fong being so nasty? He knew that Fong had been upset about him staring at his mole, but this was taking things a bit too far. To make matters worse, Wong began to laugh at what Fong had said, and the two of them were now sniggering together.

Jack was starting to feel uncomfortable. Maybe he shouldn't have taken a ride with Wong and Fong after all. The only reason he did so was because he thought Fong might be useful in gathering information about the panda. Now the two teenagers were talking to each other in Chinese, and Wong was looking at Jack in the rear-view mirror with a nasty expression on his face.

There was only one thing to do, and that was to figure out what these guys were saying. Quietly, Jack opened his Book Bag and pulled out his Secret Language Decoder. This gadget could not only listen in on conversations and translate what someone was saying into

English, it could also read foreign text. It was one of the GPF's most useful tools.

When Jack pushed the black button on the top of the silver box, a short wire with a microphone on the end popped out. He pushed some buttons which told the box to listen in on what Fong and Wong were saying and translate it from Chinese into English. As the Decoder listened, Jack watched the illuminated screen in the middle.

'We need to get rid of him,' Fong said, taking a long drag on his cigarette. 'He's smarter than I thought. He figured out the panda was taken out of the park and loaded onto a truck. It's only a matter of time before he realizes it was this one.'

When Jack heard that, his eyes bulged. He knew there was something odd about Fong and Wong, but he would never have guessed they were involved in taking Ling.

'I agree. Let's kill him.' Wong laughed.

Jack gulped.

'We can tell him we're taking him north through the park to the Great Wall,' suggested Fong. 'We can say that there is someone there who knows something about the panda.'

'Perfect,' said Wong. 'I like your plan.'

Although Jack hadn't noticed it before, he realized as he watched Wong drive that he had the same scorpion tattoo as Fong on his left hand. Fong turned round to talk to Jack as Wong continued to drive north through the reserve. Jack quickly moved the Secret Language Decoder out of the way.

'We're going to take a little drive,' he said to Jack, 'out of the park and towards the Great Wall of China. Wong says that there is someone on the way who knows about the panda. I think we should check it out.'

'Sure, Fong,' said Jack calmly,

pretending to go along with the plan. 'I'd love to meet the contact.'

Fong turned back round in his seat with a sly smile on his face. Jack looked through the window. They passed a sign which read:

YOU ARE NOW
LEAVING
THE WOLONG
NATURE
RESERVE

HAVE A NICE DAY

Jack laid the Secret Language Decoder on the seat next to him and closed his eyes. He couldn't believe this was happening. He was being hijacked by two criminals who wanted him dead. He

needed to escape from Fong and Wong
before they got to the Great Wall.

But how was Jack going to get away
from two people who were stronger than
him, and from a truck that was travelling
at fifty miles per hour? He needed to be
patient. Jack was going to have to wait for
an opportunity. He just hoped that break
would come soon.

Chapter 7:
The Opportunity

Fong, Wong and Jack travelled for a while when, out of the blue, Jack spotted another sign. It read:

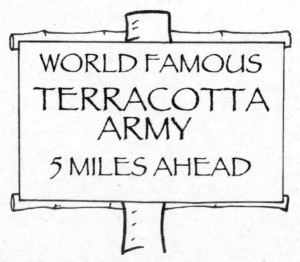

WORLD FAMOUS
TERRACOTTA
ARMY
5 MILES AHEAD

That's it! thought Jack. Just the other week, he had seen a television programme about the Terracotta Army. He knew that nearly 8,000 clay figurines made up the army and were housed in a giant museum. A perfect place to try and lose these guys, he thought.

'I've never seen the Terracotta Army before,' said Jack. 'Can we stop so that I can take a look?'

Fong looked at Wong, surprised at Jack's interest. But since Fong didn't know Jack had translated their conversation, he thought it was just an honest kid's strange request.

'Yeah, sure,' Fong said. 'We can stop for five minutes so you can see a few clay people.'

Within minutes, they'd arrived at the complex. The museum building was huge, as was the car park. After pulling in, Wong found a parking place and turned off the engine. Fong got out of the truck and pushed his seat forward to let Jack out.

'Now don't go too far, young man,' said Wong.

'Don't worry. I won't!' said Jack, strapping on his Book Bag and walking towards the main building.

But as he approached the front doors, something made Jack stop. He had the feeling that he'd forgotten something. He turned towards the truck and spotted Fong reaching into the back seat. He pulled something out and showed it to Wong. When Jack realized what it was, he panicked. It was his Secret Language Decoder.

Not only was he going to get a telling off from the GPF, it also looked like Jack was going to be in trouble with Fong and Wong. At first, the two teenagers didn't know what the strange box was, but as soon as they saw the English words on the screen, they worked it out. Jack could tell they weren't happy.

As Jack watched, Fong turned to face him. When their eyes met, Fong lifted his fists and shook them at Jack. Then the two park assistants started to run in Jack's direction.

Quickly, Jack dashed through the front doors and into the museum. Above him were several signs. One of them said 'PIT 1'. Thinking he didn't have time to be choosy, he followed the arrows. Before he knew it, he was standing on an elevated viewing platform in a massive, vaulted room.

The walkway he was standing on travelled in a square around the site, so that people could see the army from every angle. On the floor was the main army itself – 6,000 of the terracotta soldiers. As Jack stood there, wondering what to do, he heard Fong and Wong burst into the complex.

'We're going to get you, kid!' screamed Fong.

'You can't hide from us!' yelled Wong.

Jack had to act fast. The only way out of this was to go down into the pit itself, and try to lose them among the terracotta statues. Jack quickly lowered himself down. When he looked up, he found himself surrounded by some of the fiercest figures he'd ever seen.

Jack darted through the sculptures, trying to zigzag in a way that would confuse Fong and Wong. But from the

elevated platform where they were
standing, the two teenage boys could see
everything. They soon lowered themselves
down and continued the chase.

Jack stopped for a second to see where
they were. Fong and Wong were only a
few soldiers behind. He carried on moving
as quickly as he could. When he reached

the end of that section of soldiers, he
looked up. Above him was another
viewing platform.

He leaped up to the lower bar and
pulled himself onto the top of the stand.
Giving himself a moment to catch his
breath, Jack looked around for Fong and
Wong. They were just below him, trying to

pull themselves up onto the walkway too.

Jack sprinted across the platform and through the door marked 'EXIT', not stopping until he reached Fong and Wong's truck. Luckily for him they hadn't locked it, so it was easy to grab his Secret Language Decoder.

With the gadget tucked safely back into his Book Bag, Jack looked for a way to escape. Unfortunately he was too young to drive.

Just then, he spied a tour bus parked across from where he was standing. Thankfully the door of the bus was wide open.

Perfect, thought Jack.

He made a break for it, sprinting and diving through the open bus door, just as Fong and Wong burst out from the museum. Lying on the floor of the bus, Jack grabbed onto the handle that closed the door and, with one yank, sealed it shut.

Crawling commando-style along the floor down the middle of the bus, he found a hidden spot near the back. He lifted his head just enough to see Fong and Wong standing in the middle of the car park. They looked confused. No wonder – Jack was nowhere in sight.

He ducked and hid in the back for what seemed like an eternity, until he heard a

big gush of air. It was the door to the bus
– someone had opened it. Grabbing
onto the straps of his Book Bag, he
waited quietly in case it was Fong and
Wong.

'Welcome aboard, ladies and
gentlemen,' bellowed an American voice
from the front as people started piling
aboard the bus. 'I hope that you have
enjoyed your tour of the Terracotta Army.
Next stop is the Great Wall of China,' it
went on, 'and the magnificent capital city
of Beijing.'

Must be the bus driver, thought Jack.
He stayed hidden in the back, so the
driver wouldn't know he was there. As the
tourists shuffled around and found a seat
on the bus, Jack risked another look at
the car park. There was no sign of Fong,
Wong or their truck anywhere.

Although Jack didn't want to travel all

the way to Beijing, he knew that this bus was the safest place to be. There wasn't any sign of the two teenagers in the car park, but that didn't mean they weren't lurking, lying in wait for him somewhere on the main road. He settled himself in for the journey and began to think about what to do next.

He still had to find and rescue Ling, capture Fong and Wong and return the panda to the reserve. He wondered where those nasty teens were, and where they'd stashed Ling. Jack had a lot of thinking and planning to do. Time was running out.

Chapter 8:
The Great Wall

Jack took his Encryption Notebook out,
activated it with his thumb and began to
jot down some thoughts with its pen. The
GPF's Encryption Notebook cleverly
allowed secret agents to take notes and
then turn their words into code, so
criminals couldn't use the information if
they got their hands on the gadget. Jack
wrote down what had happened and the
things he noticed:

Suspects: Fong and Wong; last names unknown.

Suspect profile: Both about sixteen years old. Smokers. Both like to wear dark clothes.

Distinguishing marks: Both have scorpion tattoo on left hand. Fong has hairy mole on his chin.

Other information: Home addresses unknown.

As Jack reviewed the information, something became clear. Fong and Wong had to be part of a gang. Not only did they dress alike, they also had the same scorpion tattoo.

Gang members often tattooed themselves to show their support for each other. The fact that they both had the same tattoo was no coincidence, thought Jack. But he still wasn't sure what the gang was all about and why the two boys had stolen Ling.

One thing was for sure, and that was that Fong and Wong liked to smoke. Although smoking was a bad habit, it wasn't an odd thing to do. This made Jack remember the matchbook he'd found in the forest near where Ling was last seen. He pulled it out of his trouser pocket and looked at it closely.

It looked identical to the matchbook that Fong had tried to toss out of the truck's window – the one that flew back at Jack. The colour was the same, as was the placement of the Chinese characters on the front.

Since people often took matchbooks from whatever bar or restaurant was

offering them, Jack wondered if the one in the forest also belonged to Fong. If Jack could decipher the Chinese writing, it should tell him where Fong collected it. Then Jack could visit the place and see if it was where the two teens hung out.

As Jack carried on writing and thinking, the tour bus drove through the craggy mountains of China towards the Great Wall. In the distance, he could see the huge structure. It took over one million

people to build it and many of them lost their lives. As Jack looked at the wall, which looked like the ridged back of a sleeping dragon, he thought about what it would have been like to live in ancient China.

Even though they were now hundreds of miles away from the Terracotta Army, Jack kept a lookout for Fong and Wong through the back window. You could never tell when and where your enemy would surface.

Chapter 9:
The Clue

Placing the matchbook on the pull-down table in front of his seat, Jack grabbed his Secret Language Decoder again. Pushing the black button, he made the microphone disappear back inside. After switching it from 'listen' to 'read' mode, he waved the other end of the box over the Chinese writing on the matchbook. The Secret Language Decoder took the information and translated it into English for Jack on the screen. It said:

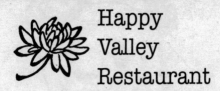

Happy Valley Restaurant

in the heart of Beijing. Delicious food at delicious prices. Dazhalan Lu Lane.

Phone: 66013269.

'Interesting,' muttered Jack. Fong had picked up this matchbook at a restaurant in the Chinese capital of Beijing. But why were they in Beijing? Perhaps, Jack reckoned, that was where they had the base for their operations. Deciding it might be a promising tip, Jack decided to stay on the bus all the way to the capital city.

Who knows – this could be my lucky break, he thought.

Chapter 10:
The Scorpion

After hours of dozing on and off, Jack
finally woke up to the loud voice of the
American bus driver.

'Here we are, ladies and gentlemen,' he
said. 'The capital city of China, Beijing.
Our first stop is Tian'anmen Square. You
have two hours to tour the square and
the Forbidden City before meeting back
here.'

As the paying passengers made their
way off the bus, Jack joined them and did

his best to blend in. Luckily for him, the bus driver was too busy making notes on his clipboard to notice Jack as he walked by.

Stepping out of the vehicle, Jack made his way over to the great square. Tian'anmen Square is the largest square in the world, well known as the entrance to the Forbidden City and as the site of a famous student protest in 1989.

He found a metal bench not too far
away and sat down. Having made a
mental note of the restaurant's address,
he pulled out the GPF's Map Mate. The
Map Mate could download satellite
images of any neighbourhood in the
world, and give you detailed maps of how
to get from one place to the next.

After Jack had punched in the address,
Dazhalan Lu Lane, and his starting
point, Tian'anmen Square, the Map
Mate created a map of his exact route.
It not only listed the streets in Chinese
and English, but also used arrows to
show him the quickest way of getting
there.

With his Map Mate to hand, Jack stood up and headed south. He walked through the plaza, under an enormous gate and onto an extremely busy road with chemists', clothing and snack shops everywhere.

After a few blocks, he turned right onto a very old and narrow road with medicine and clothing stores housed in ancient buildings. On the street itself were several vendors selling everything from Chinese dumplings and eggs to cheese and fizzy drinks.

Jack carried on along three more streets and found himself on Dazhalan Lu Lane. According to the matchbook, this was where he would find Happy Valley restaurant. Almost as soon as he started looking, he spied the place. It was the only restaurant on the lane and had pretty red Chinese lanterns hanging outside.

But as Jack approached, something else caught his eye. Next to the restaurant was a building with an interesting front window. Painted on it was a gigantic scorpion, just like the one on Fong and Wong's left hand.

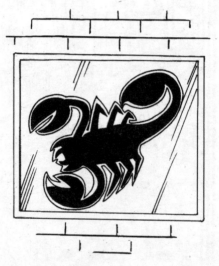

Now things were starting to make sense. If Jack was right, this was the Scorpion Gang's headquarters. And the only way to find out what was truly going on was to get inside.

Chapter 11:
The Headquarters

Keeping an eye out for Fong and Wong,
Jack peered through the window. It was
completely dark inside. It didn't look as
though anyone was there.

Trying not to draw attention to himself,
Jack slipped his hand over the door knob.
He gave it a yank, but it was locked.
Reaching into his Book Bag, he pulled out
the GPF's Magic Key Maker. After Jack had
slid the rubber tube into the key hole, it
instantly hardened, forming a key. He

looked over his shoulder for any passers-by, before turning the special key and stepping inside.

Once in, he closed the door behind him and pulled what looked like a round coin out of his shirt pocket. The coin wasn't actually a coin, but a GPF Motion Sensor that would send a signal to his Watch Phone if Fong, Wong or the other gang members returned. As he was attaching the Motion Sensor to the bottom corner of the door, he heard a noise that made him jump.

'*KACK! SQUAWK!*'

He turned round and listened again for the noise.

'*KACK! SQUAWK!*'

There it was. There was only one thing that could make that kind of sound, thought Jack, and that was a bird. He peered through the darkness and saw the eyes of a bird locked in a cage.

'I don't suppose you know what Fong and Wong are up to?' he whispered to the bird, half-jokingly, as he walked up to the cage to have a better look.

'*KACK! KACK!*' replied the bird as it flapped its wings.

Jack made his way round it and passed several other crates and coops with strange animals inside. Although he didn't recognize the first bird, he knew

some of these creatures. One was a golden monkey, a rare breed found only in China. In a large wooden crate there was a snow leopard that looked as if it had been drugged. Finally, and most surprisingly, there was a Crested Ibis, one of the rarest birds in the entire world.

Having seen these animals in their cages, Jack realized what Fong and Wong were up to. They were stealing endangered animals and selling them. That would explain why they took Ling. Since the panda would have been too big for this room, Jack reckoned she was on another level. But where? He needed to press on and look for more clues.

As Jack walked through the large room, he came to a flight of stairs. He grabbed onto the railing and climbed, taking each step slowly so the stairs wouldn't squeak.

When he reached the top of the first flight, he peered down the dark corridor to his right. At the end of the hallway he could see a small room with a television flickering. Dozing in wooden chairs in front of the TV were two teenage boys – no doubt other members of the Scorpion Gang.

Carefully climbing to the next level, Jack

found himself facing a door. Rather than
open it and risk waking the boys below,
he pulled out the GPF's Ear Amp. He
clipped the tiny device into his ear and
listened closely for any noise on the other
side. There were several things.

The first sound was of the traffic in the street below. The second was the sound of rustling grass. Finally, he could hear something chomping on food. Putting these three things together, Jack worked out that there was a rooftop terrace through the door and Ling, the Giant Panda, was probably out there eating bamboo.

Jack was facing a pretty risky situation. Somehow he had to rescue the panda without waking the boys below. He took a few moments to think of a plan and then moved towards the door to put it in motion.

Chapter 12:
The Intruders

But just as Jack was about to open the door, the Motion Sensor alarm on his Watch Phone went off. He looked down the stairs and saw the lights flicker on. Someone had entered the building. A male voice began speaking in Chinese. Jack pulled his Secret Language Decoder out of his bag.

'Get up!' said the first voice. It didn't sound like an adult's. It came from a teenager.

'Wake up, you lazy lot!' A second

teenage voice rang out. Jack recognized it as Fong's, which meant the first voice he'd heard was probably Wong's.

From where he was, Jack could hear the boys on the first level get out of their chairs. He then saw them shuffle down the steps to the ground floor, where they greeted Fong and Wong.

Fong was acting like the leader of the group, telling everyone to move the animals to a new location. Jack heard the sound of cages scraping on the floor. Then he heard the front door slam shut. The other two boys must have left the building, thought Jack, because the only voices left were those of Fong and Wong.

Knowing that Ling was probably next, Jack realized he had to get moving. Quickly, he opened the door to the roof.

Unfortunately, as it opened, it made a horrible sound that could be heard throughout the building.

SHREEEEEEEEEK!

'Who's there?' shouted Fong as he raced up the stairs in time to see Jack step out onto the roof.

'Get him!' shouted Wong as they sprinted after him.

Chapter 13:
The Preparation

Jack stepped onto the terrace and
scanned the roof. He needed to find a
way to block the door.

To his left was a statue of a Buddha, a
man who was an important religious
figure in China. The statue was heavy, so
Jack slid it in front of the wooden door.
That should hold for a few minutes, he
thought, as he heard Fong and Wong
slam into the door.

BLAM!

The Buddha statue barely moved.

BLAM!

It inched forward just a bit.

Jack's clever doorstop was only going to last a little while. He needed to get to

Ling before Fong and Wong broke the door down.

The roof terrace was filled with pots of bamboo. Guessing the panda was hidden somewhere behind them, Jack hurried over. He pushed the grass aside, calling Ling's name as he searched. Finally he spied her, sitting quietly eating her food.

'Don't worry,' he said, hoping she might understand. 'I'll save you, and take you back home to Mei.'

BLAM!

Jack looked over at the door. The statue wouldn't hold it closed for much longer. With one more push, Fong and Wong would be on the roof.

'Let's get going,' said Jack to Ling as he reached into his Book Bag. He pulled out the bits to the Heli-Spacer. The GPF's Heli-Spacer was a disc that secret agents could stand on and fly using only their hands.

Quickly, Jack assembled the gadget. He took out the disc and opened it wide enough so that both he and Ling could fit on. Then he took a steel rod called the 'prop' and snapped it into a hole on the disc. When he was ready, he pushed a button and two propellers shot out of the top of the 'prop'.

Leaving the Heli-Spacer behind, Jack dashed over to the pots of bamboo. He pulled out the GPF's Laser Burst and flicked it on. A bright white beam shot out through the tip. As Jack swiped it across the stalks, the bamboo quickly fell to the ground. Gathering as much as he could carry, he raced back to the Heli-Spacer, tying the stalks to the propeller with the belt from his trousers.

When Ling saw her bamboo, she

shuffled over and sat down on the disc. It was exactly the result that Jack was hoping for. He hooked a special rope around Ling and clipped it to the Heli-Spacer, so she wouldn't fall off.

BLAM!

Jack spun his head round. The door to the roof came crashing open. Fong and Wong were standing in the doorway fuming with anger. For a second they couldn't work out what was going on, but when they realized what Jack was doing, they hurried after him.

Chapter 14:
The Technique

Jack dived onto the Heli-Spacer and
clipped a special belt around his waist.
He pulled himself up and thrust his arms
forward as quickly as he could. The
gadget began to lift off the ground, but
not fast enough.

Fong and Wong grabbed onto Jack's
ankles and reached up to unclip his belt.
When Jack was no longer attached, they
threw him violently onto the roof. He
tumbled over a few times, coming to a

stop on his back. With Jack no longer standing on the disc to drive it, the Heli Spacer lowered itself and Ling back onto the roof.

'I'm going to get you, you punk!' shouted Fong as he glared at Jack.

'We'll show you who's boss!' snarled Wong, rubbing his fists together as though he was about to punch Jack.

The GPF always taught its secret agents to keep their cool in dangerous situations. Jack wasn't going to let these guys scare him. He crawled into a standing position.

'What do you say we finally finish this kid off?' said Wong.

'Be my guest,' replied Fong, getting ready for a fight.

As Wong reached out to grab him, Jack remembered the *harai goshi*. Since the boys were Chinese, Jack reckoned they probably hadn't practised this Japanese martial-art move before. He grabbed Wong's sleeves and moved in towards his body. Before Wong knew what was happening, Jack lifted him up on his back, grabbed his trouser leg and tossed him on the floor. As he went down, Wong banged his head on one of the bamboo pots, which knocked him out.

'Look what you did to my friend!' Fong yelled. 'I'll show you!' He took a knife out of his pocket, flicked the blade and lunged towards Jack.

But Jack was too quick. As Fong moved in, Jack grabbed his sleeves and swept his left leg across Fong's right foot. Fong started to fall, and Jack used his body weight to throw him onto his back. This was the *deashi harai*, or 'forward foot sweep'. It was one of Jack's favourite judo techniques. As Fong lay there, Jack stepped over him and stomped on his wrist, causing him to let go of the knife.

'Owww!' Fong yelled in pain, clutching his wrist with his other hand.

Jack picked up the knife, closed the blade and put it into his pocket for safe-keeping. Reaching into his Book Bag for his Net Tosser, he threw the expanding net on top of the two, trapping them underneath.

Jack phoned the local police and told them what happened. He asked them to

meet him there on the roof. By the time he'd finished on the phone, Wong had begun to wake up and Fong was crawling to his knees.

Within minutes, the police stormed the building. When they saw Ling on the roof, they frowned at Fong and Wong. Jack removed the Net Tosser so the police could handcuff the two thieves and take them away. As they were shoved towards the door, Fong and Wong looked back at Jack and sneered.

They were going away for a long time, thought Jack as he smugly waved goodbye to the duo. Harming or stealing a Giant Panda was a very bad thing to do.

A Chinese police officer came up the stairs towards Jack. He let him know that they'd caught the other two boys loading crates of animals onto a truck

from another building a few blocks away.
Jack was delighted – the Scorpion Gang
had been stopped for good.

Chapter 15:
The Wrap-Up

Rather than fly Ling back to the nature reserve, Jack figured it would be better for the panda if a van took her home. Once he'd arranged it with the police and the local animal-protection unit, he called the Wolong Nature Reserve on his Watch Phone to tell Mei the good news. He could hear her voice through the tiny speaker.

'I can't thank you enough, Secret Agent Jack, for finding Ling,' said Mei. 'Who was responsible for taking her?'

'I'm sorry to tell you, but it was your park assistant Fong and his friend Wong,' said Jack. He heard her gasp.

'They weren't exactly who they said they were,' he explained. 'They and two other boys were members of a gang that stole many animals. They were planning to sell them, and were holding them in a building here in Beijing. My bet,' Jack added, 'is that Fong worked at the reserve just to be able to take Ling.'

Jack could hear the disappointment in Mei's voice. 'That's terrible,' she said. 'I can't believe it.'

'Me neither, Mei,' said Jack. He glanced at the time. 'Well, since everything is wrapped up, I'd better sign off.'

'All right,' said Mei. 'You know you're welcome in China whenever you want to come back. And thank you again.'

'No worries,' replied Jack. 'I hope Ling

is safe from now on.' After saying
goodbye, he punched a button on his
phone and hung up.

Jack scanned the roof. The crooks were gone, the police were gone and Ling was gone. He was the only one left. He punched a few buttons on his Watch Phone and when the time was right, yelled, 'Off to England!'

Almost immediately, Jack was catapulted back home. When he arrived, he looked over at Whizzy (who was still dozing) and at his shelf in the far corner of his room. Sitting on top were trophies and framed photos from his first year of judo with Mr Baskin.

Seeing these made him smile. It wasn't a gadget that had got him out of that situation with Fong and Wong – it was his quick-thinking and judo moves. Silently, he thanked Mr Baskin for being such a good teacher.

As he changed his clothes and climbed into bed, Jack thought briefly about Charlotte, the girl who threw him to the floor doing the *harai goshi*. Little did she know he'd had some extra practice. He'd definitely be ready to face-off again next weekend. In fact, he couldn't wait.

Find out more about
Secret Agent Jack Stalwart at

www.jackstalwart.com

Great games, puzzles,
free downloads,
activities, competitions
and much more!

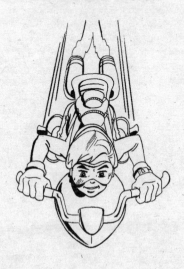

SECRET-AGENT NOTES

SECRET-AGENT NOTES

SECRET-AGENT NOTES

SECRET-AGENT NOTES

SECRET-AGENT NOTES